P9-CNC-367

Big Max in the Mystery of the Missing Moose

by Kin Platt
Pictures by Robert Lopshire

An I CAN READ Book®

Harper & Row, Publishers

 Printed in the United States of America. For information address Harper & Row, Publishers, Inc., 10 East 53rd Street, New York, N.Y. 10022. Published simultaneously in Canada by Fitzhenry & Whiteside Limited, Toronto.

Library of Congress Cataloging in Publication Data
Platt, Kin.
Big Max in the mystery of the missing moose.

(An I can read mystery)
SUMMARY: Big Max, the world's greatest detective, helps the zoo keeper find a missing moose.
[1. Mystery and detective stories] I. Lopshire, Robert. II. Title.
PZ7.P7125Bj3 [E] 76-58727
ISBN 0-06-024756-8
ISBN 0-06-024757-6 lib. bdg.

To Charles F. Mintz,
a very great detective

Big Max looked at his telephone.

"Nobody has called today," he said.

“No wonder.

The wind blew my sign over.

That will do it."

The telephone rang.

"Ha!" Big Max said. "I knew it!"

MA BELLE
ACME
MAGNIFYING
GLASSES

"Can you find a missing moose?"
a man said.
"I can find anything,"
said Big Max.
"Then find Marvin," the man said.
"It is very hard to lose a moose,"
said Big Max.
"Come to the city zoo," the man said.
"I'm on my way," said Big Max.

Big Max blew into his umbrella.
The umbrella filled with air.
"Ready for takeoff," he said.

Big Max flew through the sky.

Soon he met an airplane.

"I am looking for a missing moose,"

Big Max called.

"Sorry," the captain said.

"We don't have one with us.

We only carry people."

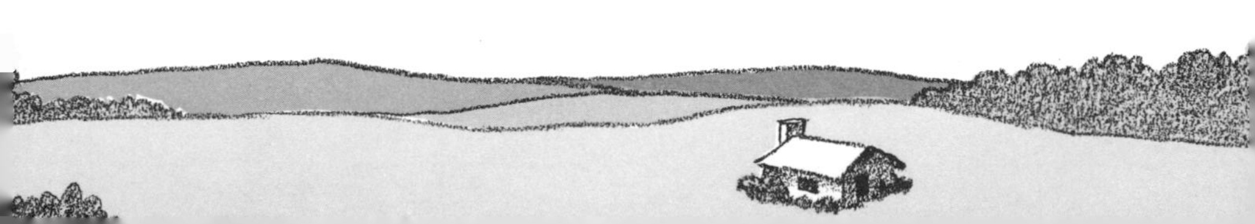

Big Max met some sea gulls.

"We are looking for fish,"

a sea gull said.

"Want to join us for breakfast?"

“No, thanks,” said Big Max.

“I am looking for a moose.”

“He doesn’t look as if he
eats that much,” a sea gull said.

CITY ZOO

Big Max flew over the city zoo.
"Prepare for landing," he yelled.

Big Max came down fast.

He landed with a bump.

"Ow!" cried a man.

"I forgot to tell you

I travel by umbrella,"

said Big Max.

"I know that now," said the man.

"I am the zoo keeper.

My name is Mr. Zonker."

"Is your moose, Marvin, lost
or stolen?" asked Big Max.
"Who would want to steal
a moose?" Mr. Zonker asked.
"Marvin can fill up a house.
Also he eats a lot.
Nobody wants that kind of pet.

We have a lot of animals here,"
Mr. Zonker said,
"from aardvarks to zebras.
But Marvin is our only moose."
"I will find him," said Big Max.

"This is Marvin's cage,"
Mr. Zonker said,
"right near the hot dog stand."
"I love hot dogs," said Big Max.
"So does Marvin," Mr. Zonker said.
"He likes his with
plenty of mustard."
"Me too," said Big Max.
"Hmm. Marvin's cage
is still locked.

MARVIN
A MOOSE
HOT DOGS

And these bars are not bent,
so Marvin did not slip out of here."
"Marvin likes to jump,"
said Mr. Zonker.
"A moose cannot jump this high,"
said Big Max. "When did you
see Marvin last?"
"Yesterday," Mr. Zonker said.
"No footprints," said Big Max.

"Marvin has found a new way
to be missing."
"You're telling me,"
said Mr. Zonker.

“Hmm,” said Big Max.

“I see peanut shells here.”

“Marvin loves peanuts too,”

said Mr. Zonker.

“That can be a clue,” said Big Max.

"Where did Marvin come from?"

asked Big Max.

"He came from way up north,

from Moose Land," Mr. Zonker said.

"Hmm," said Big Max.

Suddenly they heard

GROWWWWWWRRRRR!

"What is that?" Big Max asked.

"My lions are getting nervous,"

said Mr. Zonker.

"They don't like balloons

on windy days like this."

"I don't see any balloons,"

said Big Max.

"The balloon man is over there,"

the zoo keeper said.

LIONS

"He fills balloons with air
and sells them to the children."
"That is very nice," Big Max said.
"Not for my lions,"
Mr. Zonker said.
"They hate balloons."
"How did Marvin feel about
balloons?" asked Big Max.
"He loved them," said Mr. Zonker.

"I like to see happy children,"
said Big Max.
"They won't be happy long,"
said Mr. Zonker. "Watch!"
The children waved the balloons,
and showed them to the lions.

The wind blew harder.

It blew the balloons away.

"Come back!" the children yelled.

The lions jumped at the balloons.
Some tried to eat them.
POP POP POP POP POP!
The balloons broke,
the children cried,
and the lions began to roar,
GROWWWWWWRRRRR!
"Marvin never got mad,"
said Mr. Zonker.
"He loved the children."

Big Max looked at Marvin's cage.

It was full of balloons.

"Ha!" said Big Max.

"I know how he did it!

Come quickly!

No case is too hard,

if we look and think."

"If you don't find Marvin,

I will lose my job.

That's what *I* think,"

said Mr. Zonker.

"A moose voice is like a loud horn,"

said Big Max.

"If Marvin is around,

we will find him."

They heard a loud sound.

AH-HUMM!

They ran around the corner.

“That is not Marvin,”

said Big Max.

“That is a stuck auto horn.”

“It sure fooled me,”

said Mr. Zonker.

They heard another loud sound.

AH-HUMM-AH-HUMM!

"Stay where you are, Marvin,"

Mr. Zonker shouted.

"We're coming!"

The sound got louder.

OOM-PA-PA! OOM-PA-PA!

"It is a band concert!" said Big Max.

"Those horns can fool you."

"Perhaps you are not

such a hot detective

after all," said Mr. Zonker.

"We shall see," said Big Max.

They heard a new sound.

AH-MA-MOOOM!

They followed the sound

to the sea.

"Marvin, where are you?"
yelled the zoo keeper.
"Marvin is a smart moose,"
Big Max said.
"He left no tracks."

They heard

AH-MA-MOOOM!

Big Max found a boat.

"Follow that moose," he said.

"Aye, aye, sir," said the skipper.

Fog rolled in.

The air looked like pea soup.

"Marvin, are you there?"

Mr. Zonker shouted.

They heard the sound again.

AH-MA-MOOOM!

This time it came from the left.

"Marvin!" Mr. Zonker yelled.

"Stay put!"

The sound came from the right.

AH-MA-MOOOM!

"Marvin, stop horsing around,"

Mr. Zonker shouted.

The fog lifted.

"We were fooled," said Big Max.

"A moose has a foghorn voice.

But these were *real* foghorns."

The fog rolled in again.

CRUNNNNCHH!

"We get off here," said Big Max.

"Where are we?" asked Mr. Zonker.

"We are here," said Big Max.

“Marvin went this way,” said Big Max.

“Those are not moose tracks,”

Mr. Zonker said.

“They are sled tracks

and dog tracks.”

“I know,” said Big Max.

“Marvin is a smart moose.

He hitched a ride.”

Big Max rented a dog team
and a dog sled.
"Mush!" said Big Max.
"Marvin, I'm freezing,"
Mr. Zonker cried.
"How can you do this to me?"

"This is a frozen lake,"

said Big Max. "Marvin went this way."

"How do you know?"

asked Mr. Zonker.

"Because of that big hole,"

Big Max said.

"Marvin and the sled were too heavy.

They fell through the ice."

There was a funny sound.

CRRRRAACCKKKK!

Big Max and Mr. Zonker

fell through the ice.

“That is how Marvin did it,”

said Big Max.

“You are a great detective!”

said Mr. Zonker.

They made a fire to keep warm.
"Poor Marvin," Mr. Zonker said.
"He must be frozen stiff."
Big Max stood on a hill of snow.
"Let us think," said Big Max.
"This hill is moving.
Hills do not move.
This hill is now as high
as a polar bear," said Big Max.

“It has teeth like a polar bear.”

“AAAARRRGHHHH!”

said the hill.

“There is more proof,” Big Max said.
“We are looking for a moose,
not a polar bear.”
“Moose are that way,” roared the bear.

They came to a forest.

"Marvin must be lost,"

Mr. Zonker said.

"Call him and see," said Big Max.

Mr. Zonker yelled,

"Marvin, where are you?"

They heard a sound.

"AH-HA-HOOOM!"

"It's Marvin!" Mr. Zonker cried.

"Another case solved," said Big Max.

"Marvin," Mr. Zonker said,

"who are these other moose?"

"This is my wife," Marvin said.

"These are my two young ones.

Say hello to Mr. Zonker, family.

He is my zoo keeper."

"AH-HA-HOOOM!" they said.

"This is Big Max," Mr. Zonker said.

"He helped me find you."

"The balloons gave me the clue,"

said Big Max.

"The balloons and the wind."

"The balloons of the children
stuck in your antlers.
The wind lifted you up
and out of your cage.
The balloons flew you
to the water.
When they ran out of air,
you swam."
"You guessed it,"
said Marvin.
"But why did you do it, Marvin?"
asked Mr. Zonker.

“Marvin played with the children
at the zoo every day,”
said Big Max.
“He missed his own family.”

"Yes," Marvin said.

"You guessed right again."

"You can bring your family

to live at the zoo with you,"

said Mr. Zonker.

“What about hot dogs?”

asked Marvin.

“All you can eat,”

Mr. Zonker said.

“We’ll do it,”

said Marvin’s wife.

“Hot dogs sound terrific!”

“It’s a deal!” said Marvin.

"Big Max, how much is your

bill for finding Marvin?"

asked Mr. Zonker.

"If you don't mind,"

Big Max said,

"I'd rather be paid in hot dogs."

"I don't mind," the zoo keeper said.

Big Max took a deep breath.
His umbrella took him up.
"See you back at the zoo,"
yelled Big Max, the greatest
detective in the world.